Dear Parent:

W9-BVF-231

Psst . . . you're looking at the Super Secret Weapon of Reading. It's called comics.

STEP INTO READING® COMIC READERS are a perfect step in learning to read. They provide visual cues to the meaning of words and helpfully break out short pieces of dialogue into speech balloons.

Here are some terms commonly associated with comics:
    PANEL: A section of a comic with a box drawn around it.
    CAPTION: Narration that helps set the scene.
    SPEECH BALLOON: A bubble containing dialogue.
    GUTTER: The space between panels.

Tips for reading comics with your child:

• Have your child read the speech balloons while you read the captions.
• Ask your child: What is a character feeling? How can you tell?
• Have your child draw a comic showing what happens after the book is finished.

STEP INTO READING® COMIC READERS are designed to engage and to provide an empowering reading experience. They are also fun. The best-kept secret of comics is that they create lifelong readers. **And that will make you the real hero of the story!**

Jennifer L. Holm and Matthew Holm
Co-creators of the Babymouse and Squish series

Copyright © 2022 Hanna-Barbera.
SCOOBY-DOO and all related characters
and elements © & ™ Hanna-Barbera.
WB SHIELD: © & ™ WBEI. (s22)

Published in the United States by Random House Children's Books, a division of Penguin Random House LLC, 1745 Broadway, New York, NY 10019, and in Canada by Penguin Random House Canada Limited, Toronto. This work was originally published in different form by Scholastic Inc. as *A Merry Scary Holiday* in 2011.

Step into Reading, Random House, and the Random House colophon are registered trademarks of Penguin Random House LLC.

Visit us on the Web!
StepIntoReading.com
rhcbooks.com

Educators and librarians, for a variety of teaching tools, visit us at RHTeachersLibrarians.com

ISBN 978-0-593-64543-7 (trade) — ISBN 978-0-593-64544-4 (lib. bdg.)
ISBN 978-0-593-64545-1 (ebook)

Printed in the United States of America

10 9 8 7 6 5 4 3 2 1

SCOOBY-DOO!
SCOOBY'S SCARY CHRISTMAS!

Adapted by Lee Howard
Illustrated by Alcadia Scn

Based on the episode "A Scooby-Doo! Christmas"
by John Collier, George Doty IV, Jim Krieg,
and Ed Scharlach

Random House 🏠 New York

It is Christmas Eve. The Mystery Inc. team is going to Daphne's uncle's house.

I HOPE WE GET THERE SOON. THE SNOW IS REALLY HEAVY.

RUH-ROH!

OH, NO! THE BRIDGE IS OUT.

The Mystery Machine skids to a stop.

5

The gang goes outside. They hear loud screams.

JEEPERS! WHAT IS THAT ALL ABOUT?

CREEPY SNOWMAN! LIKE, RUN FOR YOUR LIVES!

The gang escapes! They find the town inn.

YOU SHOULD LEAVE. THAT WAS THE SNOW MONSTER.

7

DON'T LISTEN TO OLD JEB. I'M SHERIFF PERKINS. WHERE ARE YOU FOLKS GOING?

MILLS CORNER. BUT THE BRIDGE IS OUT.

YOU CAN STAY HERE AT MY INN.

CRASH!

There is a loud noise.
The gang runs outside.

HOW WILL SANTA COME NOW?

The snow monster destroyed the chimney on the little boy's house.

IT'S TIME TO CATCH THAT SNOWMAN!

They follow the snowman's tracks.

ZOINKS!

RUN!

Back at the inn . . .

HMMM . . . WHY DOES THE SNOW MONSTER DESTROY CHIMNEYS?

THIS IS PROFESSOR HIGGENSON. HE WROTE A BOOK ABOUT THE MONSTER.

11

THE SNOW MONSTER IS THE GHOST OF BLACKJACK BRODY. HE STOLE GOLD FROM SEAMUS FAGIN.

Velma reads the professor's book.

ACCORDING TO LEGEND, BRODY FROZE INSIDE A SNOWMAN. THE GOLD WAS NEVER FOUND.

Blackjack Brody

The gang starts to investigate.

THAT SNOWMAN GOES TO THE OLDEST HOUSES. I BET HE'LL LOOK HERE NEXT.

LET'S CHECK IT OUT!

The gang peeks into the house.

JEEPERS!

They hide. The snow monster goes outside.

Fred, Daphne, and Velma throw snowballs at the monster. It runs right toward . . .

. . . Shaggy and Scooby!

LIKE, THIS IS FUN!

ROARRRRR!!

The snow monster's roar cracks the ice.

CRACK!

I THINK WE LOST HIM.

RUH-ROH.

THEY ARE FROZEN LIKE POPSICLES!

The gang heads back to the inn.

I WONDER ABOUT THAT SHERIFF.

WHAT ABOUT THE INNKEEPER?

19

Fred picks up the professor's book. Daphne sees the author's name. William Fagin Higgenson!

HE MUST BE RELATED TO THE FAGIN WHO LOST HIS GOLD TO BRODY!

THAT GIVES ME AN IDEA. SCOOBY AND SHAGGY, STAY HERE. GIRLS, LET'S GO!

Shaggy and Scooby sit by the fireplace. But the fire goes out and the inn suddenly gets very cold.

UH-OH, SCOOB. HE'S BACK!

ROAR!

CRASH!

Shaggy and Scooby fall into a box of Christmas lights.

They run up to the roof.
They need to find an escape!

WA-HOO!

HANG ON, SCOOBY!

RUN FOR YOUR LIFE!

Fred's plan is to melt the snowman. They will use heat lamps.

Daphne turns them on.

OH, NO! I'M MELTING!

There is a machine inside the snowman!

LET'S SEE WHO'S INSIDE.

Velma pushes a button. The machine opens.

PROFESSOR HIGGENSON!

BRODY TOOK MY FAMILY'S GOLD AND HID IT IN A CHIMNEY. I LOOKED IN ALL THE CHIMNEYS IN TOWN. BUT ALL I FOUND WERE BRICKS.

THAT GIVES ME AN IDEA.

Velma picks up a brick. She wipes away the soot. The brick is made of pure gold!

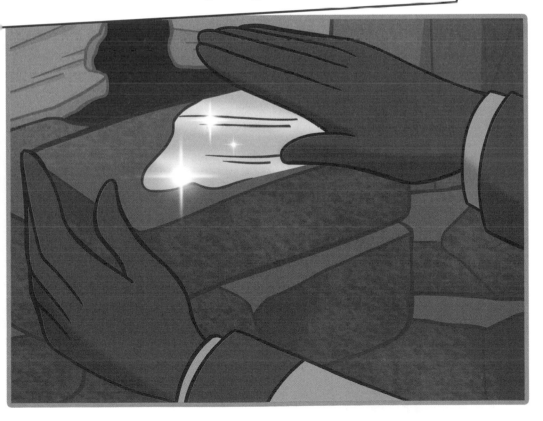

NOW I HAVE TO GO TO JAIL. I'VE LOST THE GOLD AGAIN!

CAN WE FORGIVE HIM? IT'S CHRISTMAS!

AFTER ALL I'VE DONE, YOU'RE GIVING ME A PRESENT?

I RECKON THIS GOLD IS RIGHTFULLY YOURS.

THIS GOLD BELONGS TO THE WHOLE TOWN!

31

IT'S A MERRY CHRISTMAS AFTER ALL!

ROOBY-ROOBY-ROO!

32